USBORNE FIRST LEARNING

# Starting to measure

Karen Bryant-Mole  Edited by Jenny Tyler
Illustrated by Graham Round

## About this book

This book is designed for an adult and child
to use together. It introduces children to three
areas of measurement: length, weight and capacity,
explaining and exploring the language associated with
each one. Children learn to compare objects and put
them in order according to how long they are, what
they weigh and how much they hold. They then begin
to measure using non-standard units. The book makes
a variety of suggestions for practical activities
which you can easily follow up at home.

# Notes for parents

It is best to use this book when both you and your child are in the right mood to enjoy it. Try not to do too much at any one time. If your child seems unready or unwilling to tackle any of the pages, just leave it and come back to it later.

## Length

The first pages of this book look at the comparis on of two or more objects when placed side by side. When following up with similar activities, you may need to show your child how to line up the objects along an imaginary baseline. This is important because although it is sometimes easy to tell which of two randomly placed objects is longer, the comparision is far more accurate if the objects are compared from the same starting point.

This section then looks at measuring lengths using non-standard units. The book suggests magazine pages and bricks. Other ideas include a set of felt pens, paperclips or playing cards. It is important to make sure that all the "units" are identical in size. Don't worry if your child's bed is not an exact number of pages long. It is enough to say it is "about 7".

Measuring using body units is introduced at the end of this section. You could see how many other body units you and your child can think up.

## Weight

After looking at the terms "heavy" and "light", this section concentrates on weighing using a balance. Most schools use balances to introduce children to weighing. You could make one to experiment with at home like this:

You will need: a wire coat hanger, a cotton reel*, 2 identical large yogurt pots, a circle of stiff paper, sticky tape, thin string and some playdough.

Tie the cotton reel to one end of a piece of string. Attach the other to the coat hanger as shown. Fold the circle of paper in

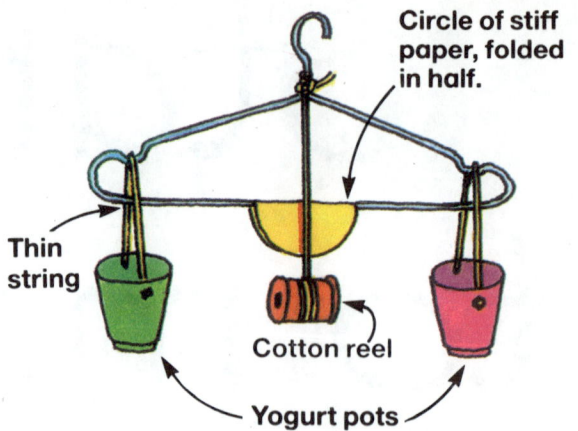

half and hang it over the bottom rail. Stick it in place and draw a line down the centre. Make a handle for each yogurt pot using equal lengths of string. Loop one over each end of the hanger. Allow the hanger to swing freely. The cotton reel and string should hang directly down the line of the paper. If not, stick a little playdough round the wire on the lighter side until the two sides balance.

## Capacity

Containers can be very deceptive. It is important to include as many practical experiences with them as you can. Most young children automatically look at the height of a container and make a judgement about its capacity on that basis. They will assume a tall, thin container will hold more than a short, fat one. Try to find two containers where this is not the case and let your child experiment by pouring water from one to the other.

You may find that your child cannot accept the results and still insists that the taller container must hold more. You cannot make him understand that this is not the case, but by providing him with lots of pouring activities you can help him reach this stage in his development.

## Following up

Measuring is a practical activity. Use this book as a starting point to look for and develop as many measuring experiences as you can in your child's everyday life.

*empty spool of thread (US)

# Who is taller?

- There are two of each type of tall animal in the safari park. Colour the taller animal in each pair.

- Who is taller, cat or mouse? Colour his hat.

- Can you find someone who is taller than you?

# Short and shorter

- Cat and mouse have lots of short friends.
- Find the shorter of each pair of animals and colour her windmill.
- Colour the shorter flower in each pair.

# Long and longer

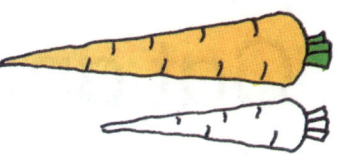

- Cat and mouse are making vegetable soup.

- They have two of each type of vegetable but they only need the longer of each pair.
  Help them by colouring the longer vegetables.

- Who has the longer knife, cat or mouse?

- Colour the saucepan with the longer handle.

# Cat and mouse's play

- Cat and mouse and their friends are performing a play.

- What story do you think they are acting out?

- Who is pretending to be Goldilocks?

- Which animals are dressed up as the three bears?

- Colour the tallest chair green.

- Colour the shortest chair red.

olour the longest bed blue.

olour the shortest bed orange.

olour the tallest bear yellow.

olour the shortest bear brown.

an you tell the story of Goldilocks and the Three Bears?

# Measuring with bricks

- Cat and mouse are using bricks to measure their furniture.

- Colour the correct number of bricks to show how long each piece of furniture is.

- Frog is measuring snail. How many bricks long is he?

# Measuring with paint cans

- Each animal is standing near a stack of paint cans.

- How many paint cans tall is dog? Colour that number of cans. Do the same for the other animals.

- Now write in the boxes below how many cans tall they all are.

- Who is the tallest? Colour his paint brush.

- Who is the shortest? Put a splash of red colour on him.

- Which two animals are the same height?

# Measuring beds

- Cat and mouse are measuring their beds with magazine pages.
- Colour in the number of pages each bed measures.

Cat's bed

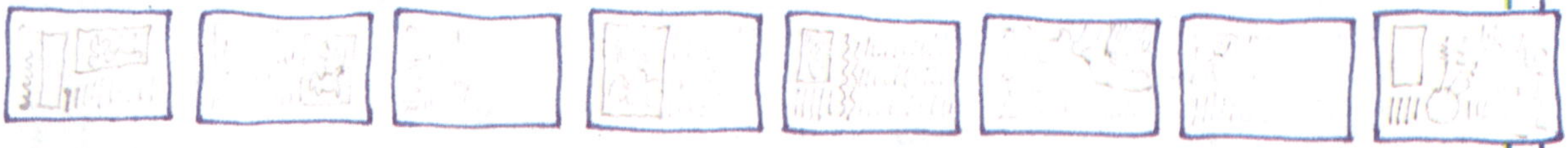

Mouse's bed

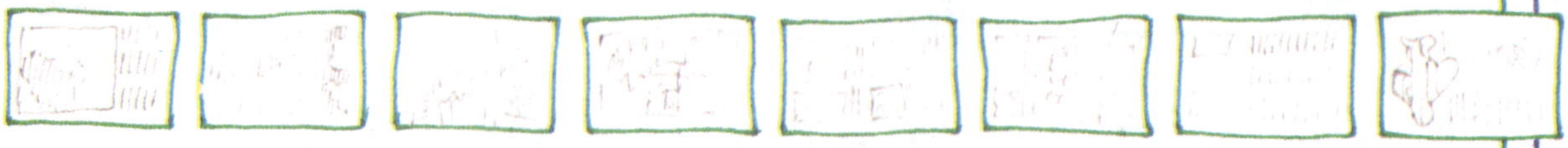

- Use pages from an old magazine to measure your bed.

My bed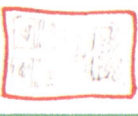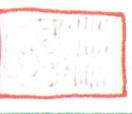

# Measuring with hands

- Cat has cut out some paw prints. He is using them to measure his door.

- How wide is cat's door? Colour in the correct number of paws.

- Measure your door with your hand. Stretch out your fingers and count how many times your hand fits across your door.

- How wide is your door? Colour the correct number of hands.

# Measuring by walking

- Mouse has made footprints in the snow. How many steps did he take to get from the house to the bird table?*

- Count how many steps you take to get across your bedroom.

- Count how many steps you take to get across your bathroom.

- Which room is longer? Choose the correct picture.

*bird feeder (US)

# Heavy and light

- Look at each thing in frog's bedroom and decide whether you think you could lift it.

- Draw a yellow star on all the heavy things you couldn't lift.

- Draw a red spot on all the light things you could lift.

- How many light things are there? ☐    • How many heavy things are there? ☐

- Are there more light things or more heavy things?

# Using balances

- Mouse is using a balance to find out which is heavier, bird's feather or spider's apple.

- A balance works like a see-saw. The thing that is heavier pushes down harder and makes its side lower than the other side.

- Which is heavier, the apple or the feather? Colour it orange.

- If the apple is heavier than the feather, the feather must be lighter than the apple. Colour the feather blue.

- The other animals are playing with things that use the same idea as a balance.

- Draw orange hats on the heavier of each pair of animals.

- Draw blue scarves on the lighter of each pair of animals.

- The next time you go on a see-saw, find out whether you are heavier or lighter than the person on the other end.

- Finish colouring the picture.

# Cat and mouse weigh things

- Cat and mouse have compared lots of things on their balance. They have put them in a row in order of weight.

- Mouse is standing near the lightest thing. Colour it green.

- Cat is standing near the heaviest thing. Colour it yellow.

- Which things are heavier than the cake?

- Which things are lighter then the slipper?

- See if you can find something which is heavier than the cake but lighter than the apple. Colour it red.

# Full and empty

- The animals are drinking orange juice after running a race.

- Draw a ring round the full glasses.

- Draw a cross on the empty glasses.

- Who is holding a glass that is neither full nor empty?

- Colour the labels of the empty bottles.

- How many full bottles are left over?

# More and less

- Look at each set of pictures and make up a story about them.

3

- Draw a ring around the bucket that holds more sand.

3

- Colour the container that holds more water green.
- Colour the container that holds less water blue.

3

- Draw a spoon in the container that holds less cake mixture.

# Match full and empty

- Cat and mouse and their friends each have a container full of water.

- They are trying to decide which empty container on the floor holds about the same as the one they are holding.

- Help them by drawing lines to join the containers that hold the same amount of water.

- Colour each empty container to match its full one.

# Cat's bath time

- Cat has lots of plastic containers to play with in the bath. He has put them in a row according to how much water they hold.

- The cup holds least. Colour it blue.

- The bucket holds the most. Colour it green.

- Which containers hold less than the red bottle? Colour them blue.

- Which containers hold more than the red bottle? Colour them green.

# Bear's birthday party

- Bear is having a birthday party.

- He has put a jug of juice on each table. There is enough juice in each jug for everyone at the table to have one cupful.

- Look at the jugs below. Work out which table each one comes from and colour in the number of cups it would fill.

- Which jug holds the most? Draw a ring around it.

- How many cups of juice does it hold?

- Which jug holds the least? Put a cross next to it.

- How many cups of juice does it hold?

# Paddling pool puzzle

- Cat, mouse and frog have used buckets to fill their pools with water.

- How many buckets did it take to fill cat's pool? ☐

- How many buckets did it take to fill mouse's pool? ☐

- How many buckets did it take to fill frog's pool? ☐

- Colour the pool that holds the most water yellow.

- Colour the pool that holds the least water green.